JESUS AND BILLY ARE OFF TO BARCELONA

Deirdre Purcell

SHORTLIST

First published in 1999 by
New Island
This Large Print edition published
2011 by AudioGO Ltd
by arrangement with
New Island

ISBN 978 1 4056 2325 4

British Library Cataloguing in Publication Data available

Printed and bound in Great Britain by
MPG Books Group Limited

CHAPTER ONE

The Cast

Our hero is Billy O'Connor from Finglas. A fair-haired schoolboy of sixteen years of age and of normal talent. He is a wee bit small for his age. And rather young-looking. He is very annoyed about this. He has long conversations with his pals about the women he has had. He fights a lot with his very irritating sister, Doreen.

*   *   *

Jesus Martinez, from Barcelona, is aged seventeen. He looks, dresses and acts a lot older. He is beautiful, with skin as velvety as a peach, curly brown hair and dark grey eyes with lashes that Liz Hurley would kill for. His parents have money, lots

1

of money. Jesus, who has lovely manners, never talks about this.

* * *

Doreen O'Connor, who is eighteen, spends most of her life worrying about being fat. Her best friend, Betty Fagan, is always telling her she is *not* fat. Doreen thinks that Betty, who is as thin as a lollipop stick, is only saying that. Doreen is feeling grim at the moment because she feels life is passing her by in the matter of boyfriends. She's never had one. Betty has had a boyfriend for a year now and this has put their relationship under strain. Doreen's also fed up with her parents because they're fixing it for Billy to go to Barcelona. A chance *she* never got.

* * *

Jimmy O'Connor, thirty-nine years of age, the father of Billy and

2

Doreen, works in Premier Dairies. He is a cheerful sort, happy with small joys. Likes the odd pint. He is proud of his family, proud of his little house. Proud that, with his own hands, he can keep the old family banger on the road. The only fly in the ointment is that his wife, Janet, keeps nagging at him to do courses so he can get a better job. Jimmy is glad to have the job he has. No hassle, no stress.

*   *   *

Janet O'Connor, Jimmy's wife, loves her children. She loves Jimmy too, but is at an age where suddenly none of that seems enough. She finds herself looking at holiday programmes on the telly. Janet's main question now is: why can't Jimmy O'Connor get up off his arse and get himself a better job? She has great plans for her children and has taken on extra ironing shifts down at

ValuKleen, the local laundromat.

*   *   *

Granny Teresa, who is seventy, is Jimmy's mother. She lives with the O'Connors in a little granny flat stuck on to the side of the house. She is a terrific granny, warm, wise, motherly.

*   *   *

No one can guess the age of Amanda O'Connor (no relation) because she keeps herself so well. The gym, tennis, the odd facial—well, you have to, don't you? Amanda lives with Hugo, her husband, on the south side of the city in a keyhole cul-de-sac of lovely houses. All with different shapes. Amanda has high ambitions for her only son, William. She doesn't want him to be a dull old accountant like Hugo, who works all the hours God sends. William has

4

always been good with his hands so maybe he would be a surgeon.

*　　　*　　　*

There are other people in this story, such as Billy's uncle Dick, who also lives with the Finglas O'Connors and who is sozzled most weekends.

*　　　*　　　*

But finally—the person without whom we wouldn't have a story at all.

*　　　*　　　*

Sharon Byrne is twenty-two and has lovely hair. She also has lovely nails and lovely ankles and a heavy DART accent. Her Daddy always said that Sharon was good with people so she did a PR diploma at a private college. Unfortunately, PR didn't work out for her, so when she saw a summer job advertised in Irlanda

5

Exchange, she thought she'd give it a whirl.

Sharon has been with The Agency for all of six weeks when the trouble she has to face on that August Bank Holiday weekend makes her think yet again about her line of work . . .

CHAPTER TWO

Billy Prepares to Meet Jesus

The jury was still out on Billy O'Connor's family. Billy sometimes thought they were not too bad. Like on certain Sundays when his Uncle Dick was too sick to come downstairs. His mother, who always saw this as a blessing, would behave like a real mother. Like the mothers you see on the telly. Jolly. The kind of mother who cracks jokes about the burnt corned beef and is so relaxed about it that everyone is allowed to laugh.

Sometimes, on the other hand, Billy thought he was going to die of shame because he was forced to live on the same planet as these people. Not to speak of in the same house on the same street.

At the moment, he was in between.

On the good side, it was very good of his parents to go to all the trouble and expense of arranging this student exchange with the bloke from Barcelona. Billy's scholarship covered only half the cost, so to pay for the rest of it, his Da had done lots of overtime. He had also borrowed from the Credit Union. His Ma had taken on extra work down at ValuKleen.

On the bad side, they never let Billy forget their goodness. Billy only had to do one thing. One small tiny thing (like forgetting to put out the milk bottles on one single night) and they were all off. He was an ungrateful little pup who had no idea what the real world was like. *He* didn't have to wear the same pair of laddered tights for a month. *He* didn't have to suck up to that shagger Moreno down at the plant in order to scrounge a few bloody hours of extra work on a Saturday night.

When they first told him about the

trip, about three months ago, he had been excited. But then, the next day, when he thought about it, he became a bit afraid too.

It was all very well watching Barcelona on Sky and slagging off Rivaldo and Figo. Or laughing about the poxy Spanish food they must eat in Spain. But then you remembered that soon you'd have to eat the same poxy food. Billy hadn't had the courage to ask anyone to tell him stuff about Barcelona. Billy was in the habit of pretending to know things.

What was most on his mind was that he might make a fool of himself with the Spanish women.

Billy was worrying about women right now, as a matter of fact. Lying on his bed on top of his Liverpool F.C. sleeping-bag, he was worrying not only about Spanish women but about all women. If worrying about women was an Olympic sport, Billy O'Connor would have walked it.

He looked at his watch. Only three hours before they were due to go to the airport to meet his exchange partner who had this weird name.

Jesus.

Imagine calling your son Jesus, Billy thought. It certainly wouldn't work here. A Finglas Jesus wouldn't dare to show his face outside the door.

In another part of the house, he could hear Granny Teresa crackling at something someone said on a re-run of *The Golden Girls*. Listening to her, Billy smiled. Granny Teresa was alright, actually. She was the only one in the house who liked Kung Fu films. And although it wasn't really cool to admit that you loved your grandmother, in his secret heart, Billy glowed when he was around her.

He envied her in a sort of a way too because she was seventy and, therefore, everyone had to respect her. She didn't have to give a sugar

10

about his Ma's moods or her PMT. And any time his Da got stroppy she'd shut him up with a look and ask him who did he think he was. That she used to change his nappy.

His Uncle Dick—now there was another kettle of kippers. Dick was the Black Sheep of the entire family on both sides. He was separated. He'd had to go back to live with Granny Teresa only four years after he was married. Then the two of them came to live with Billy's family when Uncle Dick drank them both out of house and home and they had nowhere else to go.

The problem with having Dick in the house was that no one could sleep with him because he snored like an elephant. So he had to have a bedroom all to himself. But there were only three bedrooms in the house proper. So Dick got one. There was one for his parents and one left for Doreen. So Billy had to sleep on a sofa bed in what his Da liked to call The Conservatory.

For the next three weeks, Jesus was going to be in Dick's room and Dick was going to be sleeping with Granny Teresa in the granny flat. The rules from the agency said that Jesus had to have a room of his own.

The Conservatory was a lean-to glasshouse. Billy's Da had bought it cheaply from someone in Rush who was getting out of market gardening. His Da 'borrowed' a milk float from Premier Dairies and one Saturday morning, he, a mate of his, and Billy had gone to collect it. They had to hurry and get the float back to the plant before that shagger Moreno missed it.

Billy didn't mind because, as a bedroom, it wasn't too bad actually. Once he got used to the brightness, birds in the morning, that sort of thing, Billy got to quite like it.

He checked his watch again. Two hours and fifty minutes to go. He settled down with a dog-eared copy of *Playboy* magazine. His friend, Anthony, had got it from a bloke he worked with on the building site. Now that Billy was sixteen years old, his Ma and Da didn't bother taking stuff like *Playboy* away from him any more. He hoped this Jesus was as into women as he was.

CHAPTER THREE

Sharon Gets a Puncture

'Bloody hell!' Sharon Bryne swore as the steering wheel of the Polo shuddered and then became heavy between her hands. (She had wanted a Golf but her Daddy wouldn't rise to it. The old meanie.)

She had a puncture.

Of all the days!

Sharon had been driving down Monkstown Avenue in a thick stream of traffic. She heaved at the steering wheel to get the car neatly into the kerb. She glared at the furious face of the Beemer driver who passed her making rude finger signs. All right, so she hadn't indicated. Big deal. She stuck out her tongue at him as she put on her flashers.

One by one, the honking cars swerved out and drove past her.

Calm down, Sharon, she said to herself. Just ring the AA first. Then ring Jackie and tell her you'll be there as quickly as you can.

Thank God for mobiles, she thought.

Making sure she did not break her fingernail, she carefully tapped in the AA breakdown number. She always kept it safely taped to the dashboard of the Polo. She was kept waiting, of course. She had to listen to bloody Enya. What was it about Enya? She was everywhere. Poodle music, Sharon called it. Sharon herself was into heavier music, like Blur.

After what seemed like a week, the AA woman came on. Took the details. Then—disaster! The wait would be an hour or probably more.

'An hour?' Sharon couldn't believe it. This was an emergency. She tried to explain to the woman how much of an emergency this was. But the woman explained back to her that because this was a Bank Holiday

15

Friday, there was murder on the roads. She'd do her best, the woman said, but she couldn't promise help sooner than an hour. Click. The woman was gone.

Sharon thought for a moment. Then tapped again on her mobile.

Damn! Daddy's mobile was off.

It wasn't fair. She just felt like getting out of the Polo altogether and walking away. She felt like crying. She nearly did, actually, but then she pulled herself together. Stop this, Sharon, she said sternly to herself. Don't be such a baby. You're in a grown-up job. Behave like a grown-up.

She frowned. Sharon Bryne was not going to be beaten by this. She tapped in Jackie's number

'Oh my God—!' Jackie's voice could barely be heard above the noise all around her. She was in the arrivals hall at the airport. 'Sharon, you can't do this to me. You just *can't*. You *have* to come

16

immediately. Get a taxi, all right? The company will pay. Just come *now*. You should be here already—' The connection was broken and Sharon was left holding the stupid dead mobile in her hand.

This was dreadful. The silly woman was demanding that she should abandon the Polo? Just leave it here for robbers and lowlifes?

She took three deep breaths to calm herself down. Brigitte, who gave Sharon and her mother Ki-Massage, had taught the two of them how to slow the body down. It always worked. After the third breath, Sharon was no longer upset.

She tapped in Daddy's mobile number again. Still off.

All right. She was on her own here. She would leave the Polo and get a taxi. But first she would ring AA and tell them they'd have to tow it for her to a garage. They'd do that. They'd have to. Sharon's family paid squillions to them every year for the very top cover.

Twenty minutes later, Sharon was driven in her taxi past the Frascati Shopping Centre. She was quite pleased with how she had handled matters. She saw she was clutching her clipboard as though it was a life-belt. Tension. Brigitte certainly would not have approved of that! So Sharon took three more deep breaths and settled back in her seat for the ride to the airport. She wouldn't think any negative thoughts. The Polo would be fine. She had put the light around it as Brigitte had taught her.

She didn't remember that she had left a file on the Polo's back seat.

CHAPTER FOUR

Jesus Flies In

Jesus leaned forward in his seat and stared through the oval window as the jet at last broke through the cloud cover. The fields around Dublin airport spread out beneath it like a bright green-and-white tablecloth. All around him was the excited buzz of chatter and loud talk. Jesus had no wish to be part of it. He had no friends on this trip and he was contented about that. Three weeks in Ireland with a family he did not know was fine with him.

To prepare for the visit, he had read a lot about Ireland. About Riverdance and Gerry Adams and Bono and computers. And most of all, about the craic and the Guinness and the little fairy-sized churches and the green, green grass.

And now here it was, all starting. Jesus, who never showed any excitement because to do so would be vulgar, felt a little flutter somewhere around his middle. He sat back. The flight attendant, who was passing along to check seat belts, shot him a big toothy smile. Jesus smiled back. It was good to be coming to Ireland, to escape the summer heat of Barcelona. All that endless, tiring, boring sunshine. It rained a lot in Ireland. Jesus liked rain, the way it rushed from the sky to cool the streets and freshen the flowers.

His Mama had not wanted him to come. Lately, Jesus had been finding that he and his Mama were not seeing eye-to-eye the way they used to. His brother, Jose Manuel, who was married and six years older than Jesus, had helped to persuade their Mama. Jose Manuel had said that a little holiday away from one another would be no bad thing for either of them.

His Papa did not care one way or the other. Between the polo, the bank and the club, his Papa cared little about anything to do with the family. So long as they were clothed and fed and didn't cause scandal or crash any of the cars. His Papa had no idea that Jesus knew all about the mistress he kept in an airy house near the summit of Tibidabo— the cool, wooded mountains which watched over the city.

Jesus was past caring what his Papa did.

He preferred not to remember the yelling and the screaming he had overheard from the safety of his first-floor apartment on the evening the mistress had come to the house to confront his Mama. The mistress was demanding her rightful share of his Papa's wealth.

Jesus shuddered a little now as the memory came to the surface. To push it back down again, he concentrated hard on looking at this watery land which was rushing up to meet the wheels of the jet. He could see puddles now, tiny cows, a ribbon of road, a fence and then the runway. He closed his eyes, waited for the thump and squeal . . .

His fellow students clapped and cheered.

Jesus had arrived in Ireland.

CHAPTER FIVE

Amanda and William Get Lost on the Way to the Airport

'I just don't believe this.' Amanda stared at the wasteland of shops. Many of them had strong steel bars across their windows.

'How could this have happened?' she moaned. 'I've been to the airport to collect your father a hundred times. I *couldn't* have taken a wrong turn!'

She leaned across, took a map of the city out of the glove compartment and rustled it open.

William, hot and fat in the leather seat beside her, slumped deeper and closed his eyes. His Walkman already blared into his ears but he turned it up further. He hated this. He didn't want an exchange student. He didn't want to go to Barcelona. All he wanted was to be left alone in peace in his own nice quiet room with his Playstation and his catalogues.

William collected catalogues. It didn't matter what they sold. Toys. Time-Past Celtic candles. Fishing tackle. They were all great. He filed his catalogues in big box files.

He became hooked on the hobby when his desk partner at school brought in a gun catalogue he had found in the boot of his father's car.

William could not explain why he liked this hobby so much. It sang at him, like a mermaid on a rock. When he was busy with his filing, he felt peaceful and at one with the world.

Beside William now, Amanda sighed heavily. She pressed the window button beside her seat.

The glass purred into the door frame.

Amanda called out to a group of young men who were holding up the walls on both sides of the entrance to a bookie's shop. 'Excuse me—?'

The young men looked at one another and then back at Amanda. No one moved.

Amanda was in no mood for nonsense. 'Ex-cuse me,' she yelled again. 'Could you tell me which way to go to get to the airport?'

One of the young men came slowly across to the car. 'Which airport?' he said. The others sniggered.

Amanda pressed the window button again, crashed the gears and, in a serious temper now, drove off. She pulled the headphones off William's head.

'William,' she snapped. 'Concentrate. Roll down your window and look up at the sky. See if you can see any aeroplanes . . .'

*　　　*　　　*

Doreen was giving out the pay. She and her friend, Betty, were waiting at the corner of Del Delios, the local chipper. They had both ordered singles. Doreen knew well she shouldn't be having chips. She was on a special banana-and-grape diet

25

she had read about in the *Evening Herald*. But the smell coming from the chipper as she and Betty had walked past had driven her mad.

Of course Betty could eat chips until they came out her ears. She could eat lard straight off a pig's back and not gain an ounce. Betty went to visit her auntie once in Glasgow and came back full of stories about eating deep-fried battered Mars bars. Sometimes Doreen could kick Betty from here to Glasnevin.

'If this Jesus thinks I'm going to be nice to him,' she said, 'he has another think coming.

'And how come that little brat gets to go to Spain? How come I've never been in an aeroplane in my life and I'm the oldest?'

'I don't blame you, Dor.' Betty was full of sympathy. 'Bloody Spanish students. Take over, they do. Every summer. Don't know why they come here at all, to tell you the truth. Like a flock of bloody magpies they are.

You can't even get *near* the door of McDonald's . . .'

*　　　*　　　*

Sharon stopped dead when she saw the crowd inside the arrivals building. It was *murder*. The whole of Dublin seemed to have brought its kids here on a day out.

Babies cried. Toddlers screeched as they swung on barriers and made slides on the tiled floor. Nuns. Priests. Grannies. Bored teenagers. Dads clacking car-keys.

All faced the glass doors which separated the arrivals area from the customs mall.

She saw from the arrivals board that there was only one flight on the screen which did not have a star flashing beside it. *Seven* charter flights from Spain had just landed. Plus two from Italy. Not to speak of all the Ryanairs. And Aer Linguses. And some flights which had come

27

from places with names Sharon had seen only as labels on handbags.

Sharon nearly cried. She just wanted to get back home to her nice quiet house in Dun Laoghaire. Not for the first time today, she was beginning to think that she might not be cut out for this job after all.

She nodded to a pony-tailed drug dealer whom she knew slightly.

Searching for Jackie's bright blonde head, she pushed her way along the edges of the crowd. She was here now and she had to get on with it. Irlanda Exchange was relying on her. She gripped her clipboard tightly and tried to put on what she hoped was a confident expression.

At last! She sighed with relief as she spotted Jackie, standing at a little counter, sipping from a paper cup.

'Thank God!' Jackie threw back the coffee as Sharon reached her. 'Coffee?'

Without waiting for an answer, Jackie left Sharon and went up to the counter. The girl who was serving took her order immediately. Over the heads of the people already standing there. It was like a miracle.

Sharon, too rattled to tell Jackie that she would have liked some milk and sugar, took a sip of the scalding, bitter liquid. 'Where's Norma?' she asked.

'Over there.' Jackie waved an arm. 'Her Italians are already in, she's sorting them out.'

Sharon turned around and caught a brief glimpse of Norma's frizzy black hair and purple jacket in the middle of a huge group of dark-skinned young people. She had no time to wave because Jackie had grabbed the clipboard from her.

Jackie riffled through the papers. 'Now,' she said briskly, 'let's divide our own little parcels into two neat lots, shall we?'

'Oh—!' She looked at Sharon. 'Where's your family file?'

Sharon went pale.

CHAPTER SIX

Sharon Does the Business

When the first colourful, chattering group of Spanish students came through the glass doors, Jackie and Sharon were still not ready for them. They'd been frantically working. They'd been trying to make up for the loss of Sharon's missing file by using Jackie's master list. Now it was too late.

Wave after wave of the students came through now. They poured into the space between the doors and the barriers. Packing it tightly.

'Right,' said Jackie grimly, 'we'll just have to do our best.'

Sharon felt like running away. She'd never handle this.

But she was given no opportunity to bolt.

'You go over to the other side, do

what I do.'

Immediately, Jackie held up her printed sign and began to yell. 'Irlanda Exchange! Irlanda Exchange!'

Sharon looked in terror towards the crowd of students who were trying to fit themselves through two small exit corridors between the barriers. She swallowed hard. She held up her own sign and attempted to copy Jackie. 'Irlanda Exchange?' But it came out wrong, like a timid question.

She cleared her throat. 'Irlanda Exchange!' To her relief, a number of the students noticed her and began to make their way towards her.

The next fifteen minutes or so passed in a blur of writing, shouting, crowding, as Sharon matched names of students to names of host families and had them meet. She was still only halfway through her list, however, when her eye was caught by a really handsome youth.

31

This youth was standing back as though waiting for the lesser beings in front of him to be herded away. His brown curly hair shone with health. He was not as dark-skinned as most of the others. In the middle of the sweaty crowd, he appeared as cool as if he had just stepped ashore from a yacht.

Sharon made her way to him. '*Buenos Dias*,' she said in Spanish, 'name please?'

'Jesus Martinez,' said the youth.

Sharon searched her list. 'From where? *Donde?*'

'Catalonia.'

'Catalonia?' Sharon was taken aback. 'I'm afraid you're with the wrong group,' she said slowly, making sure every word was clear. 'You need to go over there to Norma. She's the girl with the purple jacket. You see her over there?' She pointed. 'Norma's taking care of Italy.'

She turned to the next student.

But the boy wasn't going away. 'Excuse me?'

'Yes?' Sharon was a teeny bit sharp. He was cool but not *that* cool.

The boy either didn't or wouldn't react. 'Excuse me,' he repeated calmly. 'I think there is mistake. Catalonia is not in Italy. Is my country. I am from Barcelona.'

Sharon covered up. She laughed. 'Oh—! Oh, I *see*—Barcel-*ona*! What am I *thinking* of? I'm so sorry. What's the name again?'

'Jesus Martinez.'

As she ran through the 'M's on her list, Sharon became conscious of the boy's large eyes, his long lips, the smoothness of his skin. Come to think of it, she thought, he looked quite like River Phoenix. Except for the colouring and the curly hair.

At last she found his name on the list.

'Ah yes,' she said. 'You are with the O'Connors. Come this way.'

Billy was totally pissed off. The tape in his Walkman had broken and a piece of it had wound itself around the works inside. He wasn't able to fish it out properly because of all the pushing and shoving that was going on around him.

And being this long in the company of his family with no possibility of escape was terrible.

He was sure that this Jesus was going to be a dweeb. And anyway, how was he going to bring someone named Jesus around with him? It was going to be pure torture. He'd be a laughing stock with his friends. He was sorry he ever heard of Barcelona. He didn't want to go to Barcelona. He hated Spain. He hated this airport. He hated the way Granny Teresa kept saying: 'I wonder would that be him, now? He looks like a Jesus.'

He hated his Ma's bright

expression and his Da's pretend air of eagerness.

He wished he was an orphan.

'Mr and Mrs O'Connor! Mr and Mrs O'Connor—?'

There was that stupid girl with the stupid accent calling them now. She was waving at them to come over. This was it

This was the end of Billy's *life* . . .

CHAPTER SEVEN

Billy Meets Jesus

Janet O'Connor looked at the young man standing beside Sharon Byrne. 'That can't be him,' she hissed at her husband.

'She called us, didn't she—?' Jimmy wanted to get this over with.

'But he's much better-looking than that picture they gave us. He looks a lot older—' Janet was still doubtful.

Jimmy was having none of it. 'You know what passport pictures are like. Come on, will you? I'm sick of this place. Billy, Granny Teresa!' Jimmy rounded them all up. 'He's here.'

'Check out that leather coat—' Granny Teresa was whispering as though she was in the chapel. 'If I was only fifty years younger!'

They got there.

Sharon smiled brightly at the

O'Connors. 'Is William with you?' Then she turned sharply to a thin boy of about fourteen or fifteen who was tugging at her sleeve. 'Sorry?' she said. 'Yes, this is Irlanda Exchange, but you'll have to wait until I get to you, I'm very busy. I'll be with you in a moment. Please stand over there.'

But this boy, who had bad skin and dyed blond hair, wouldn't go. He continued to stand there as Jimmy spoke in that posh tone he sometimes used and which Billy hated. 'Yass,' said Jimmy. 'Oh yass.'

He pulled Billy by the arm and presented him to Sharon as though Billy was a prize in a raffle. 'Here he is!'

Billy looked at the floor.

But Sharon was not talking directly to him. 'William, meet your exchange partner. Jesus, this is William.'

All of them except Billy noticed that she pronounced Jesus as Kay-soos.

All Billy noticed was that his

exchange partner was a good ten inches taller than himself. He hunched further down into the collar of his anorak.

'Hello . . . Kaysus . . .' Janet said, speaking very slowly. 'You're . . . very . . . welcome . . . to . . . Ireland.'

Then, in a low voice to Sharon, 'We call our son Billy, actually.'

'Thank you very much, Mrs O'Connor,' Jesus said. Then he turned to Billy.

'Hello, Billy.' He held out his hand. Billy shook it then took back his hand and shoved it in his pocket.

Janet stared. 'Your English is very good.'

The boy shrugged and might have replied but Sharon wanted to move on to next business.

'Sorry, Mr and Mrs O'Connor,' she said. 'Would love to chat, but I'm sure you all want to get home and get to know one another. You have the phone numbers? We'll be in touch.'

Then, to Jesus: 'Have a nice

time now, Jesus, sorry about that Catalonia thing, it's all a bit hectic, as you can see . . .'

She turned away, raising her voice. 'Carlos Sanchez, please. Where are the Lynchs?'

The boy with the bad skin and dyed hair tugged at her sleeve again. Sharon turned on him. *'Please!* I asked you before! Stand over *there*!'

She was gone.

Jimmy looked at Jesus' luggage, piled high around his feet. 'Well, Kaysus,' he said, 'would you look at all this stuff! Did you think you were moving here or what? And I see you even have your guitar. But where's the castanets?'

Janet interrupted. *'Jimmy!'*

She turned to their guest. 'Sorry Kaysus,' she said. 'My husband is a bit of a joker.'

Jesus smiled at both of the adults. 'Of course. I bring only my guitar—'

'It's my little joke,' Jimmy laughed. 'You're not to mind me, Kaysus.'

The boy frowned. 'Mind?'

'We'll explain all that kind of thing later, Kaysus,' said Janet. 'But your English is great,' she added quickly. 'Isn't it, Billy? *Great!* We were told you'd hardly any English. I don't know why you had to come here at all.' She laughed.

Billy was disgusted. She was making her laugh sound like sleigh bells.

Billy's heart sank under the weight of shame as his family went on making shows of themselves. There was his Ma, still laughing in that sickening way as she introduced Granny Teresa. And even Granny Teresa seemed struck dumb. They were all reacting to this guy as though he was a film star. Which, Billy had to admit to himself, might not be too far off the mark.

Then Jesus presented Billy's Ma with a small packet, beautifully wrapped in gold foil and tied with silver ribbon: 'This is for you, Mrs

O'Connor, from my mother in Barcelona.'

Of course this nearly sent Billy's Ma into orbit. Her hands were holding her throat and her voice went so high that Billy thought she might as well be trying out for a Joe Dolan album. 'For me?' she squeaked.

Luckily, Billy's Da had had enough. 'Let's get out of here, Jan. This place gives me the heebie-jeebies.'

But Billy's Ma wouldn't stop. She went for the Oscar: 'Oh *God* . . . This is too *much*.'

Billy wanted to strangle her.

'Please,' Jesus said back to her, 'it is small gift only.'

Then Jesus turned to Billy. 'Our gift to you, Billy, I have in my luggage—'

Billy managed to say thanks without making a fool of himself. 'Come on,' he said. He grabbed Jesus' guitar and led the way towards

41

the doors. He was sure that, at this point, the guy must think they were all nuts.

Billy was trying to show him that there was at least one person in the group who was halfway normal.

CHAPTER EIGHT

Amanda and William Meet Their Jesus

Amanda had had to circle and circle in that damned car park. Then she'd almost come to blows with another motorist who'd claimed a space she said she had seen first.

In the end, she and William had had to park miles from the terminals. Then they'd had to run all the way to the arrivals building.

She thought crossly that this wouldn't have happened if Hugo had seen fit to come with them, as Hugo had reserved parking.

Panting hard, she pushed her way through the crowd, towards the arrivals board.

Amanda was annoyed at herself for being seen like this in public. She was sure she must look awful. Red-faced and puffing.

Heavens! She was now worried. The flight had landed more than forty minutes ago.

Amanda stood on tiptoe and searched in and around the sea of clattering heads. Thank God! There it was. The Irlanda Exchange placard.

Firmly holding William's arm, she made her way towards the placard. It was being held by an odd-looking boy whose hair was dyed to the colour of dandelions. Standing beside him was a girl with a clipboard who seemed to be in charge.

'Excuse me.' Amanda adopted her firmest tone. 'Could you assist us please? We're a little late, I'm afraid, but our name is O'Connor and we are to meet a boy named Martinez.'

The girl with the clipboard frowned as though trying to remember something. She scanned the papers on the clipboard. 'What's your boy's first name?' she asked.

Then, with feeling, 'I'm afraid Martinez is a very common name in Spain!'

'Our boy's name is Jesus,' said Amanda, pronouncing it the correct way of course. She and Hugo had long ago got over the silliness Irish people went on with when they came across the name.

'I am Jesus.' Unexpectedly, the boy with the brassy hair spoke up. Sharon turned around to him: 'You are Jesus? Jesus Martinez?'

The boy nodded.

Jesus, William, Sharon and Amanda all looked at one another.

Amanda turned to Sharon. 'He doesn't look like his photograph,' she said.

'I colour my hair yesterday,' said Jesus.

*　　　*　　　*

Out in the airport car park, Janet gave her husband a puck: 'I saw that kind

45

of luggage in a magazine, Jimmy. It's real leather. Do you have any idea how much this costs?'

Jimmy, a case in each hand, was cool. 'So what? Leather is very cheap in Spain. Don't they kill all those bulls? They have to do *something* with the skins. Anyway, he probably borrowed them.'

Janet continued to worry: 'And look at that coat. That didn't fall off the back of any lorry . . .'

'Will you stop? He could have borrowed that too—isn't he on a scholarship, just like Billy?'

'Yeah, but look at him,' Janet hissed. 'God knows what he's used to.'

'For Christ's sake, Janet,' Jimmy was working up a nice head of steam, 'it's not his fault he's so good-looking. Poor people can be good-looking too, you know.'

But Janet wasn't paying attention. 'I wish you'd listened to me about doing up that porch. What's he going to think? Thank God we at least got the new wallpaper for that box room. But it's too small, Jimmy. We should have put him in our room.'

'What?' No one, but *no one* ran down Jimmy O'Connor's house. 'We're as good as anyone, and so is our house.'

Janet interrupted: 'Listen, you bring him and Billy into town. Tell him you just want to give him a quick tour, like. I'll get a taxi straight home and sort it.'

Jimmy nearly exploded. 'No way, Jose. No way. He's coming home to Tara Downs with us and that's that. And he's coming now.'

Janet sighed. But she knew that Jimmy had put his foot down.

She walked ahead of him. 'Not far now, Kaysus. Tell me about your mother. Does she work outside the home?'

*   *   *

47

Billy stole a serious, daylight look at Jesus as they all trekked through the car park. The guy even walked like a film star. Loped.

Suddenly Billy began to feel uneasy. Beside such style and beauty, he himself was the only one who might seem like a dweeb.

At least the sun was shining. That was pretty good. To his surprise, Billy found he would have hated it if it had been raining.

He took another look at his guest. He hated to admit it, but so far Jesus wasn't half-bad. Maybe even a bit cool. Maybe having him around might not be so awful. Maybe going to Barcelona might be all right after all . . .

Suddenly, he wanted Jesus to like Ireland. To like him.

'I look forward to many conversations with you, Billy.' As though he had heard Billy's thoughts, Jesus turned to him.

'Yeah,' said Billy. And then, when

he realised that that might sound rude, 'I mean, of course, I'm looking forward to it too.'

Then he found he actually meant it.

He meant it even more when he opened the present Jesus gave him. A pair of Boss jeans. Billy's Ma only got a poxy bottle of lavender water.

CHAPTER NINE

Amanda Smells a Rat

The Saturday of the August Bank Holiday had always been a day that Amanda had secretly liked. Starting early on the Friday afternoon, all their friends did things for the holiday. They fought the traffic to West Cork, for instance (and then, all weekend, dreaded the fight home on the Monday evening). But she and Hugo had long ago decided that they would use the time quietly at home.

Anyway, Hugo always had work to catch up on. He liked the thought that for one bloody day, at least, he wouldn't be disturbed.

Knowing this, Amanda hesitated outside the closed door of Hugo's study. The house was so quiet she could hear the soft clicking of Hugo's keyboard. Then she set her lips in a firm line. This was an emergency. She opened the door and crept inside.

The curtains were pulled against the glare of the bright sunlight outside. Hugo's neck was stretched like that of a goose as he peered at the screen in front of him.

Amanda waited.

Still the clicking continued. He hadn't noticed she was there.

She cleared her throat. Then: 'Sorry to disturb you, Pet. Could I have a quick word?'

Hugo stopped clicking and looked around. His face was as cross as a ferret's. 'What is it, Pet? Can't you see I'm busy? One bloody day, that's all I ask. One bloody day in the year.'

'I know that, Pet.' Amanda stood firm. 'But this is important. It concerns William and his exchange partner.'

Amanda's husband threw up his hands in the air. 'One bloody day.'

He swivelled in his leather chair to face his wife. 'So what is it that's so important?'

Amanda took a deep breath. She had rehearsed what she was going to say. She sat down in a chair beside the desk and learned forward earnestly.

'Now, you know me, Hugo,' she began, 'I'm not one to complain. But I'm just a teeny bit worried about this Spanish lad. I mean we were *assured*—I went to a lot of trouble, Hugo, *you know* I did—that he'd fit in. We were also told, if you remember, that he had very good English?'

Amanda shook her head sadly. 'Well I'm afraid that's not the case, Hugo. That's not the case at all. I'm afraid the poor child can barely string one word after the other. "I am Jesus Martinez. I am from Spain. I colour my hair." That seems to be about it. Young William is already saying there's no way, no *way*, Hugo, that he's going back to Barcelona with this lad. And you know what that'll mean. We've already promised to go to that thingy in the Med with the Frasers. Where'll we get a minder for three weeks at this short notice? And another thing—'

Amanda hurried now because she could see her time was nearly up. 'Now, you know, Hugo, that I'm not a snob. You *know* that, Hugo. But you also know what they're like down at that tennis club. We *did* ask him to bring whites. For his own sake.'

She sat back. 'Not a sign, I'm afraid. A few grotty t-shirts, that's all. I know it's not the child's fault or anything. But, I mean, not to put a tooth in it, I think we've been sold a pup.'

Amanda's husband stared at her. 'So what do you want from me?'

Amanda stared back frankly. 'Would it be OK with you, Pet, if I called the agency? Not that we'll send him back or anything like that.

Of course not. But I just think it's not good enough. They'll have to do *something* for us.'

Hugo shrugged. Then, 'Can I go back to work now, please?'

Amanda smiled. 'Thank you, Pet. That's settled then, I'm glad you agree. Right. I won't disturb you any longer.'

As soon as she closed the door, she heard the fury of clicks from inside.

In another part of the house, the dandelion-haired Jesus Martinez sat beside William at the console of William's Playstation.

This Jesus was in heaven.

CHAPTER TEN

Jesus Scores

Saturday morning in the Finglas O'Connors was very different to Saturday morning in the southside O'Connors. Here all was go.

Billy's Ma had put a tablecloth on the table and had brought a carton of Tropicana, the posh orange juice, instead of the Squeez they usually had. She had make-up on too and her hair was done up in a pair of combs.

Billy's Da was reading the racing pages. He kept looking at Billy's Ma in a very odd way, as if he didn't know who this woman was. But then again, he did seem to like what he saw.

Doreen, who never put a foot to the floor before two o'clock any other Saturday, was up and dressed in her tightest jeans. She was weird too. 'Let me help you that, Ma.' And 'Will I pour the tea now, Ma?'

Billy knew it was all because of Jesus.

Billy's exchange partner sat quite relaxed at the table while the two women fussed around him. He was dressed in smart Levis and a navy cotton jumper which showed up the smoothness of his neck. The air in the kitchen smelled like lemons.

Then the last straw came for Billy. Doreen leaned over so far while pouring tea for Jesus, Billy thought she might fall over.

He also suspected she had put cotton wool in her bra.

'Will I go and call Uncle Dick for breakfast?' Billy asked loudly.

It was a nasty thing to do. But what the hell.

He had the satisfaction of seeing the two women turn pale. 'Ah no,' his Ma said, really quickly. 'Sure it's Saturday. Let the poor man sleep on a bit.' His Ma then turned back to Jesus: 'So what are you two lads going to get up to today?'

Jesus turned to Billy, a question mark written on his face.

Billy shrugged.

'Have you any ideas what they could do, Doreen?' Billy's Ma turned to her daughter.

'Please, no worry for me.' Jesus dipped his dry toast into his tea as he smiled around at everyone. 'I do not mind. I do with Billy what Billy does every Saturday, no?'

No one wanted to be the first to say that what Billy did every Saturday was to stay in bed.

It was decided between them all that Jesus and Billy would go into town. Billy was to take Jesus all around Temple Bar and show him the new Dublin that everyone was talking about. Jimmy slipped Billy a fiver so he could treat Jesus to a burger in Thunder Bar. He even said he'd give them a lift as far as the bus stop.

After they left, Granny Teresa went back into the granny flat, bringing a cup of strong black coffee in to Uncle Dick.

Janet and Doreen became a little thoughtful. Janet decided that it was about time she had a bit of colour put in her hair: 'For the summer, like . . .'

Doreen stared at her. Doreen told her mother that she thought she shouldn't waste her money. That her hair was quite nice the way it was. She offered to put a few rollers in it for her.

She looked away. As for herself, she said, she might wander into town. She had a few shillings to spend. She might have a look at Thunder Bar. She'd heard a lot about it.

'That's great,' Janet said.

Before either could say anything more, there was a knock on the front door. Janet sighed. 'There's a pound coin in my purse on the hall table,' she said and turned away to the sink. They had a pools man who called to the door every Saturday morning.

Doreen sighed: 'Why do I always have to go?'

She was back in less than a minute. And she had Sharon Byrne with her.

CHAPTER ELEVEN

Jesus Stays Put

'I knew it was too good to be true.' Doreen removed the cotton-wool pads from her bra. The wires under the cups were killing her. She didn't care that Sharon saw what she was doing. She didn't care about anything.

All right, their Jesus was two years younger than her. So what? Had no one ever heard of Joan Collins?

'What's the other chap like?' Doreen heard her mother's question through a fog of temper. Who cared what he was like? No matter what he was like, he certainly couldn't be like their Jesus. She stopped herself. The sad fact was that he was no longer their Jesus.

She told her mother and Sharon that she was going upstairs and left the kitchen.

Sharon watched Doreen go. As the sound of tramping feet on the stairs died away, she turned back to Janet.

'What's he like?' she said.

'He's—he's very nice actually,' Janet replied. She made her voice sound strong. 'He's *very* nice. He has a great personality,' she added hopefully. 'He even dyed his hair the night before he came here. Little scamp. Isn't that marvellous?'

'That little fella with the pimples and the brassy hair?' Janet was horrified.

Sharon bravely looked straight back at her. 'I think you probably have the right one,' she said. 'But I think that the dyed hair shows that he's really interesting, don't you? He really stood out from the crowd at the airport yesterday, didn't he?'

Then, as Janet continued to stare, Sharon rushed on. 'If you like, I'll help you pack Jesus' things, so that when he gets back from town we'll be all set.'

'Hold on a minute,' Janet frowned. 'Where's the other fella now?'

Sharon tried to keep her face bright. 'Oh, he knows all about it,' she said. 'He's really looking forward to coming to meet you all.'

The other Jesus knew about it all right but he was far from happy. His bag at his feet, he sat sadly in the room in which he had slept for just one night. He was waiting for the Mama to call him down to get in the car to go to the other family.

He kicked the bag. It had been too good to be true. Nothing ever worked out for him. Nothing.

When he had been offered the exchange scholarship, he had held his breath for a whole week in case someone would come and tell him it was all a mistake. Then, finally, when no one did, he dared to hope. He let himself believe that for once in his life, luck was with him.

He had been stupid to believe that. Stupid, stupid, stupid.

Although the Mama had dressed up the story by telling him that the family he was really supposed to be with was lovely and that he would have a lot in common with them, Jesus knew the real story. He wasn't good enough for this grand house, for these grand people.

He sighed, then decided he might as well behave as they expected him to behave. Why not?

His gaze fell on the remote control for the television. This would be exactly what they expected him to nick.

So he walked across to it, picked it up and put it in the big front pocket of his hooded anorak.

* * *

Billy and Jesus came out of Thunder Bar and into the noise and racket of the street outside where buses revved their engines and drills tore into the road.

Jesus linked Billy. 'I think we are friends, yes?'

'Of course.' Billy felt uncomfortable. 'Er—men don't link each other in Ireland,' he said, pulling his arm away.

Jesus was immediately sorry. 'I do not know all this. You must teach me.' He smiled again, a brilliant smile which set fires in his eyes.

Billy could not resist him. 'Of course I will, Jesus,' he said earnestly. 'I'll teach you everything.'

Jesus took Billy at his word and by the time they were getting off the bus at their stop, Billy was explaining the differences between the Premiership league and the league run by the Football Association of Ireland. He summed it up for Jesus in one sentence. 'Basically,' he said, 'the F.A.I. is crap.'

Then he had to explain what 'crap' meant.

As they strolled home from the bus stop, Billy basked in the smiles and admiring glances Jesus got from people they passed. Billy was delighted with himself. How could he have been so stupid as to be worried about this exchange? It was working out perfectly. Jesus was probably the coolest guy Billy had ever met.

They were getting on so well that the shock when they got into the house was all the more.

The first thing they saw was the pile of Jesus' luggage. Then they saw Sharon.

'There's been a bit of a mix-up, Jesus,' said Sharon in that voice that Billy hated. 'It's just as well we found out quickly, before you got too settled here.' She laughed, a tinkly, false laugh. 'But not to worry, it's all sorted now. . .'

*   *   *

Fifteen minutes later, Sharon was no

longer laughing. Jesus, seated at the kitchen table, smiling his gorgeous smile, would not be moved. 'I like it here,' he said politely for what to Sharon seemed like the twentieth time. 'I like Billy. If necessary, I pay the other O'Connors so I can stay here with Billy.'

Doreen, who now wished she hadn't removed the cotton wool from her bra, clapped her hands as though she were at a cabaret. Janet and Jimmy both beamed. Everyone was really chuffed that such a wonderful boy would choose their gaff over a rich gaff on the southside.

Sharon swallowed hard and wished she had Brigitte beside her to tell her what to do.

'Leave it with me,' she said.

Of course as soon as she said that they all knew they'd won.

'Jesus is going nowhere,' said Billy.

CHAPTER TWELVE

How Jesus Affects the Finglas O'Connors

So Jesus stayed put with the Finglas O'Connors.

As for the other poor Jesus, he found himself packed off home to Barcelona. Amanda, naturally, had missed the remote control within seconds of entering his room.

Amanda planned to get Hugo to sue Irlanda Exchange. When he could find the time, of course. What was most urgent now was to find a minder for William for the three weeks she and Hugo were going to be away in the Med on that thingy with the Frasers.

The Finglas O'Connors cared not a fig about Amanda, or Hugo, or William. They planned to throw a big party for Jesus, to thank him for his faith in them.

The only fly in the ointment about this plan was Uncle Dick. They were a bit worried about how Jesus would feel about Uncle Dick when Uncle Dick got into his stride at the party. But then, on Jimmy's advice, they decided to hell with it. Jesus had taken them all at face value so far, hadn't he? He could take Uncle Dick's party-self as well.

To celebrate, Jimmy put his hand in his pocket again and gave Billy another few bob. This time so that he and Jesus could go to Father Moran's Friday Night Disco at the youth club.

The next few days were taken up with preparations for the party, which was to be held on the following Saturday night. Janet begged and borrowed glasses from all the neighbours. She baked buns and cakes and started hard-boiling eggs for sandwiches.

But she started doing something

unusual as well. She had always been the first up in the household but now she took to coming into the kitchen a little later than all the others. Not simply coming in, but making a sort of an entrance. Yawning sleepily and stretching her arms above her head. And saying she'd had lovely dreams. And that she wished she could go back to sleep and have another one.

And instead of her nice, comfy, fluffy dressing-gown with the rabbit on the pocket, she had started to wear the shiny one with tiger stripes that Doreen and Billy had bought her for Christmas. She'd stay in the dressing-gown all morning, only getting dressed around noon.

And Billy noticed that she was now doing everything slower. Walking slower, talking slower, even looking slower at people. She seemed to look a lot at Jesus.

Over those few days too, Billy noticed that his father, usually so easy-going, started to complain

69

about little things. He'd glare at Janet. His tea was too strong. The collar on his shirt wasn't ironed properly. What was wrong with this house? He couldn't find two matching socks.

Everyone, of course, took it out on Billy as usual.

Billy was puzzled. The whole feeling of the house had changed. Instead of being happy-go-lucky and rubbing along together, everyone, bit by bit, seemed to get more and more edgy.

Doreen, in particular, became bad-tempered, snappy with her mother.

Janet was snappy with Jimmy.

Billy even heard Granny Teresa snap at his mother when Janet asked Granny Teresa to help move the furniture around in the sitting room.

The furniture was fine the way it was, Granny Teresa had said with her nose in the air. She was having no more to do with any of this messing that was going on.

Billy was puzzled. What messing?

The only person who sailed through the days was Jesus. He didn't seem to notice that people were tense. He was the perfect guest. Helping Janet with the washing up. Leaving his bedroom in applepie order every morning. Walking with Billy to the local shops to buy sliced pans for the sandwiches. Even insisting on buying flowers for Billy's mother to thank her for going to all this trouble.

Which had made Janet go all misty, saying she hadn't had flowers since she was a girl.

Billy had to admit that Jesus was brilliant outside too. He proved to be great at football and basketball and was immediately in demand for all sport on the road. Even Anthony Murphy, Billy's best friend, fell in love with Jesus and wasn't a bit jealous that Billy had to hang around with him.

No, it did Billy no harm at all that

he was the one who had this star living in his house.

As for his family, Billy put it all down to nerves about the party. They hadn't had a party in their house since Granny Teresa and Uncle Dick had come to live with them.

CHAPTER THIRTEEN

Jesus Goes to a Disco

Anthony, who was the DJ for the night, waved at Jesus and Billy as soon as they came in. 'This next one,' he yelled, 'is for Mary and Decco who are celebrating their four-month anniversary.'

Father Moran, who was running the disco, came up to him, and put his mouth as close as possible to Anthony's right ear. 'Have you got anything in your collection that could make our foreign guests feel at home?'

Jesus wasn't the only Spaniard in the hall. There were several others, a few Italians and one lone, bored English boy. The student-exchange business was beginning to take off in the area.

Father Moran pulled back a little

from Anthony's ear. 'Maybe one of the Eurovisions?'

Anthony, afraid that anyone might hear this, jumped back as though avoiding a wasp. 'Ah no, Father,' he said, 'but if you hang on, I think I have the very thing.' He rooted around and came up with a CD single. 'Here it is, Father.' Then, raising his voice again: 'Hey—HEY! YAY! AMIGOS! WOWEE!'

As the first notes of 'La Macarena' thundered down the hall, Billy dug Jesus in the ribs. 'You have to get up, Jesus.' Billy was anxious that his personal Spaniard wouldn't let the side down. He pointed to Doreen who was hanging around with a bunch of her snotty friends near the stage and trying to look careless.

'This is a good one to ask Doreen up for,' Billy went on. 'You won't even have to touch her in this one.'

Two hours later, Doreen was frustrated. She had danced with Jesus. Her friends had danced with Jesus. But they all agreed that, beautiful and all as he was, not one of them could shift him.

He wasn't cold or boring or anything like that. 'It's just like he isn't *there* or something,' Doreen's friend, Betty, had said. Betty was free for the night because her boyfriend was away.

Now Doreen had managed to get Jesus outside. She wanted a smoke and he had been too polite to refuse to go with her. She looked up at him. 'They're all kids in there,' she said. 'Why don't we hop down to the chipper? I could murder a long ray and a single.'

Jesus looked puzzled. 'Murder?'

Doreen sighed. 'Never mind,' she said.

'I tell Billy that—'

'Told him Kaysus,' corrected Doreen. 'You *told* him—'

'I *told* him I go outside with you for your cigarette only. You are finished your cigarette now. I am very cold. Is very cold evening. Please, we go inside?'

Doreen sighed again. She tried one last time. 'Only if you dance with me again?'

'Of course.' Jesus frowned. 'But everyone ask—*is asking*—me to dance. I must not refuse, no? Is not *polite*?'

Doreen looked hard at him. 'Sometimes, Kaysus, I don't know whether or not you're taking the piss.'

'Taking the piss?' Jesus frowned again. 'I do not understand this taking the—'

'Oh for God's sake, have it your own way.' Doreen stomped off, sulking. She'd had enough. He could go to hell.

Jesus followed her inside.

Inside, there was a lull in the music. Billy, who was sucking Coca-Cola through a straw from a can, saw Jesus come in. 'Over here, Jesus,' he called.

Jesus walked over. 'Billy, we go home, soon, please?'

'It's a quarter-to-twelve,' Billy replied. 'It'll be over in fifteen minutes. Do you want a packet of crisps?'

They were interrupted by Father Moran. 'How're ye lads? Enjoying it? Some great women here tonight, eh—what?'

His next words were drowned out as 'Never Ever' from All Saints boomed from the loudspeakers.

'That's a great song altogether,' Father Moran yelled happily. 'I really dig the Spice Girls. Go on now, the pair of ye.' He slapped both of them on their backs. 'There's not much time left for ye to click—eh? Shoo! Out there now, out—out of my sight.'

Jesus followed Billy on to the dance floor. ' "Click"? Billy, what means this "click"?'

CHAPTER FOURTEEN

Jesus Gives Billy a Shock

It was after one in the morning.

Jesus and Billy were sitting on the sofa in the sitting room, which was already decorated with paper chains for the party. Billy had nicked some vodka out of the party supplies. The two of them were drinking it mixed with Coca-Cola as they watched a Don Johnson video.

They hadn't turned the main light on, and the glow from the table lamp on the coffee table in front of the fireplace made the room look cosy.

Jesus sipped his drink. 'We do not have dances like this in Barcelona,' he said. 'I hope you will not be disappointed.'

Billy smiled happily. 'Ireland's a kip. I can't wait. This video is crap.' He stood up. 'I'm starving, do you

79

want chips? I can make some, or we could go back out to the chipper?'

Jesus pretended to groan. 'Always food. Everyone in Ireland eat all the time—'

'*Eats.*' Billy, who was turning off the telly and the video, had got used to correcting Jesus' English. 'You say "*eats*".'

'Eats,' repeated Jesus, 'yes. Thank you. But no thank you, I would not like to eat chips now.'

'Oh all right,' Billy replied cheerfully. 'I'll just go into the kitchen. Ma'll have left something out for us. But its probably a feckin' *salad*. Thanks to you, ya dork!' He thumped Jesus playfully on the arm as he passed him by.

But Jesus sprang to his feet and, laughing, thumped him back and before Billy knew it, they were locked together, wrestling, giggling, pretend-fighting.

Until suddenly, Billy found himself on the sofa underneath Jesus with

Jesus' face very close to his.

They stopped fighting. Billy was feeling very, very strange. All kinds of feelings raced up and down inside him. In the course of a second or two, he felt excited, caught, embarrassed, curious, afraid, ashamed, excited again. Most of all excited.

Billy knew that he should get up. He should shove Jesus aside and get out from under him. He could laugh it off then. They could both laugh it off. But he didn't move. Jesus' breath felt warm. It smelled sweet.

Jesus very gently kissed Billy.

'What the HELL is going on here?'

Over Jesus' shoulder, Billy saw Jimmy's appalled face framed in the doorway. In the dim light, it looked like a Hallowe'en mask.

His father snapped on the main light as Billy scrambled out from beneath Jesus.

Jesus didn't seem put out at all.

'Good evening, Mr O'Connor,' he said politely. 'We were—' He hesitated as he searched for the right word.

'Janet!' screamed Jimmy.

CHAPTER FIFTEEN

Jesus Never Explains

Within seconds, Doreen and Janet were standing, gaping into the sitting room. Jimmy, who was purple in the face, could not string two words together.

Billy wanted to cry like a baby except he was frightened that if he did something awful might happen.

The only one who kept his cool was Jesus. He shrugged. What was the big deal, his expression seemed to say.

At last Jimmy managed to get a few words to come out of his mouth. 'Get to—get to bed—you—' His hand was shaking as he pointed first to Billy and then out towards the conservatory.

Billy ran past him, afraid of getting a box, although Jimmy had never in his life raised a hand to either of his children.

'As for you—' Jimmy turned to Jesus: 'As for you . . .'

Words failed him again. 'You deal with it,' he yelled at Janet. Then Jimmy ran upstairs.

Janet, in jim-jams and still half asleep, turned to Doreen. 'Was it the vodka that upset him or what?'

Doreen glared at Jesus. 'No, mother,' she said, ice dripping from every word. 'It wasn't the vodka.' She grabbed Janet's arm and pulled her away from the door and up the stairs.

Jesus, who still wore an expression of polite surprise, was left alone in the sitting room. He sat back down on the sofa as the sounds of hell broke through the house from the floor upstairs.

He took another sip of his vodka

CHAPTER SIXTEEN

Sharon Sorts It

Next morning, when Sharon and Jackie arrived on the doorstep of the Finglas O'Connors, Billy was nowhere to be seen. Jimmy had woken him early. He had dragged him out of The Conservatory, into the car and down the country to a cousin of Granny Teresa's. He was to stay there for a week. No arguments.

Janet, frozen-faced, answered the door to Sharon's ring. Behind her, Jesus' posh luggage was piled in a neat heap. 'Don't talk. Just get him out of here,' Janet said.

Sharon, whose faith in Brigitte was taking a beating (putting the light around any of these people had been a waste of time), stepped inside the hall door and took up the first suitcase.

CHAPTER SEVENTEEN

What Jesus Left Behind

So Billy never got off to Barcelona and after Jesus' departure life went back to normal.

But not quite.

Billy became moody, even moodier then he was before Jesus came into their lives. He couldn't talk about women any more without remembering the odd, strange sweetness of Jesus' kiss.

Anthony got fed up with him. And after a few weeks of seeing him moping around, Granny Teresa had had enough too. She put Father Moran on the case.

Father Moran made things worse. Father Moran's solution was that Billy should join *An Óige* and get out into God's clear mountain air. He talked about every boy feeling mixed up at Billy's age and told him he would grow out of it

The problem was, Billy had no idea whether or not he wanted to grow out of it. He couldn't care less that Anthony had dumped him. Because now he thought Anthony's talk about *Playboy* magazine and Pamela Anderson and all the rest of it was just plain childish. Having walked on the wild side, Billy wanted none of that kiddy crap anymore.

But he did take up Father Moran's offer to allow him to use the computer at the parish house. Like all his pals, Billy knew how to access the Internet and, as soon as Father Moran left him alone, he found a site for 'Barcelona'. Trying to imagine where Jesus lived, he took a virtual tour of all the tourist sights.

Then he got into a temper. It looked lovely. He could have been there. He could have been sitting in the sunshine with Jesus. He could have been sipping real drinks instead of the gunge they served at the Youth Club. He could have been swimming on golden sands and meeting Spanish women in their bikinis.

The problem was, he didn't know who to blame. Or how to feel about women in their bikinis. Much as he hated to admit it, Father Moran was right. Everything was all mixed up.

Day by day, Billy's temper got worse. Someone was to blame, that was for sure.

Because he couldn't pin the blame on anyone without thinking dreadful thoughts about Jesus, Billy took to his bed in the conservatory for the rest of the summer. He ate there, slept there and came out only to go to the bathroom. Everyone would have been worried about him if they hadn't been feeling terrible themselves.

Take Doreen. Doreen secretly confided in Betty that she knew now for sure that she'd never get a boyfriend. Otherwise, why wasn't she able to straighten Jesus out? She had had him under the same roof, hadn't she? Living with him night and day.

It was no use Betty consoling her and telling her that of course she'd get a boyfriend, that everyone did, sooner or later. Doreen just shot Betty a filthy look, walked straight into the chipper and ordered herself a batter-burger and a large single.

And then there was Janet. Jimmy would look up sometimes and catch her watching him with narrowed eyes. 'What's the matter?' he'd ask.

What he would get for his pains would be a complaint about the colour of his tie. Or why couldn't he smarten up a bit? Get his hair cut. Throw out those old shoes, for God's sake . . .

Poor Jimmy couldn't talk to anyone about anything. Especially about the gap in his heart where his marriage used to be. He took to going to the pub instead of coming home to face the closed-up expression in his wife's eyes.

As for Granny Teresa, she stopped singing around the house and could often be found sitting in a chair and staring into space. The odd time Billy and she talked to one another, both knew that the word 'Barcelona' could not be mentioned. Yet Billy's non-trip to Barcelona always lay between them like a wet sheep.

Everybody had changed.

All except Uncle Dick of course. As a matter of fact, Uncle Dick was the only person in Billy's story who was exactly the same as he was before Jesus came to Finglas.

Except Jesus, of course.

JESUS AND BILLY ARE
OFF TO BARCELONA